For Mum, Dad, Chris
and everyone else.

First published in 2013 by Nosy Crow Ltd

The Crow's Nest, 10a Lant Street

London SE1 1QR

www.nosycrow.com

ISBN 978 0 85763 199 2 (HB)

Nosy Crow and associated logos are trademarks and/or registered trademarks
of Nosy Crow Ltd.

Text and illustration © Elys Dolan 2013

The right of Elys Dolan to be identified as the author
and illustrator of this work has been asserted.

A CIP catalogue record for this book is available
from the British Library.

Printed in China

1 3 5 7 9 8 6 4 2

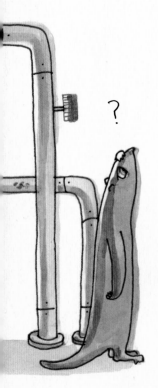

Weasels...

... what do you think they do all day?

Eat nuts and
berries?

Frolic in
the leaves?

Lurk in
the dark?

Argue with
squirrels?

Hide in their
weasel holes?

Well, all
of these
are wrong.

What they
really
do is ...

And today they take over the world.

But something has gone very badly wrong.

Who turned the
lights out?

Was that supposed
to happen?

Why is there a wet
patch here?

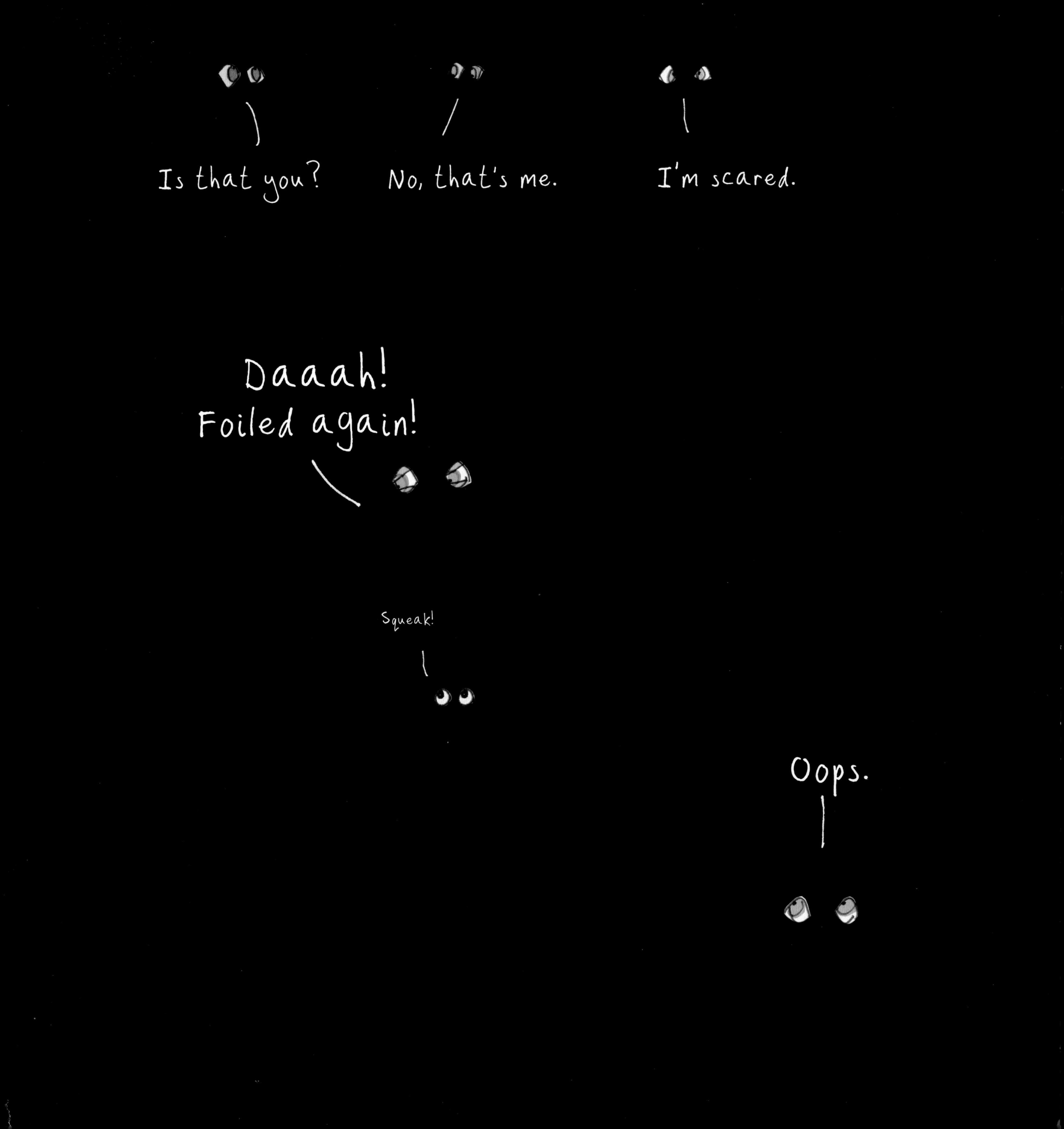
Is that you?
No, that's me.
I'm scared.
Daaah!
Foiled again!
Squeak!
Oops.

In the control room it seems that there
are a few technical difficulties.

But technical difficulties won't stop a weasel . . .

...though they do like to stick to the rules.

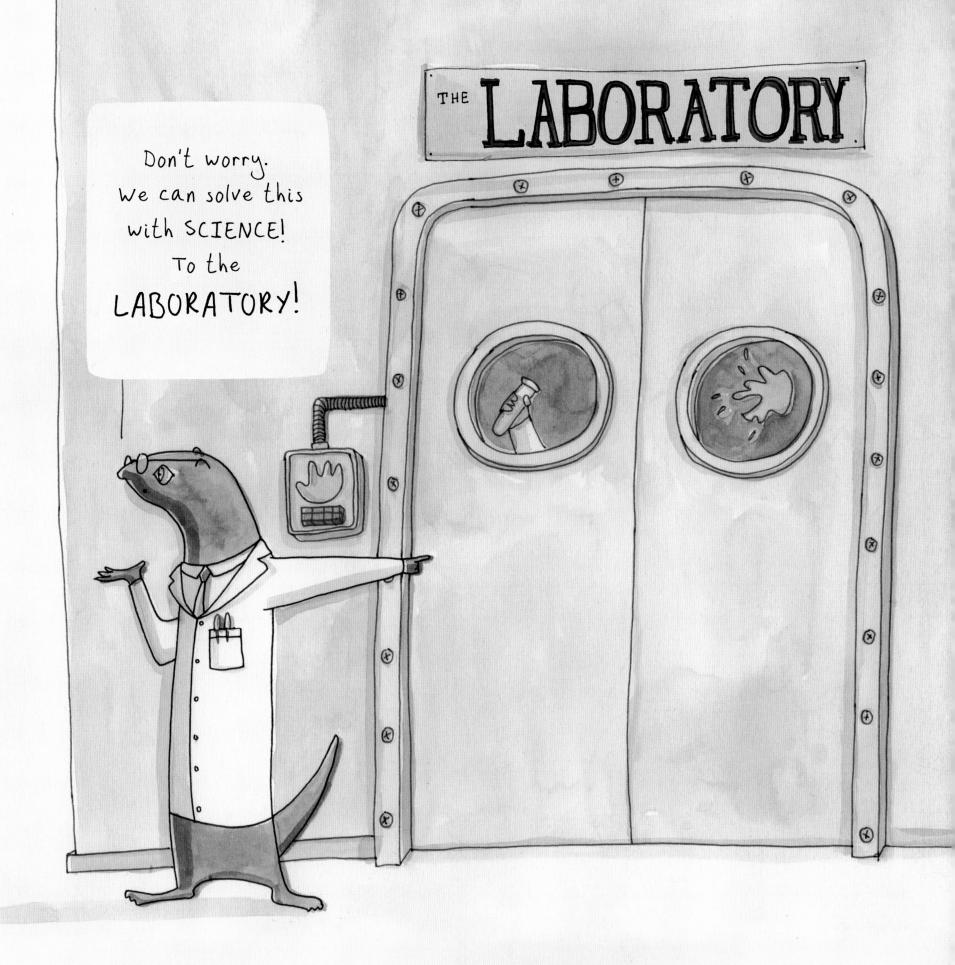

But back at the machine, things are still in chaos. What could the problem be?

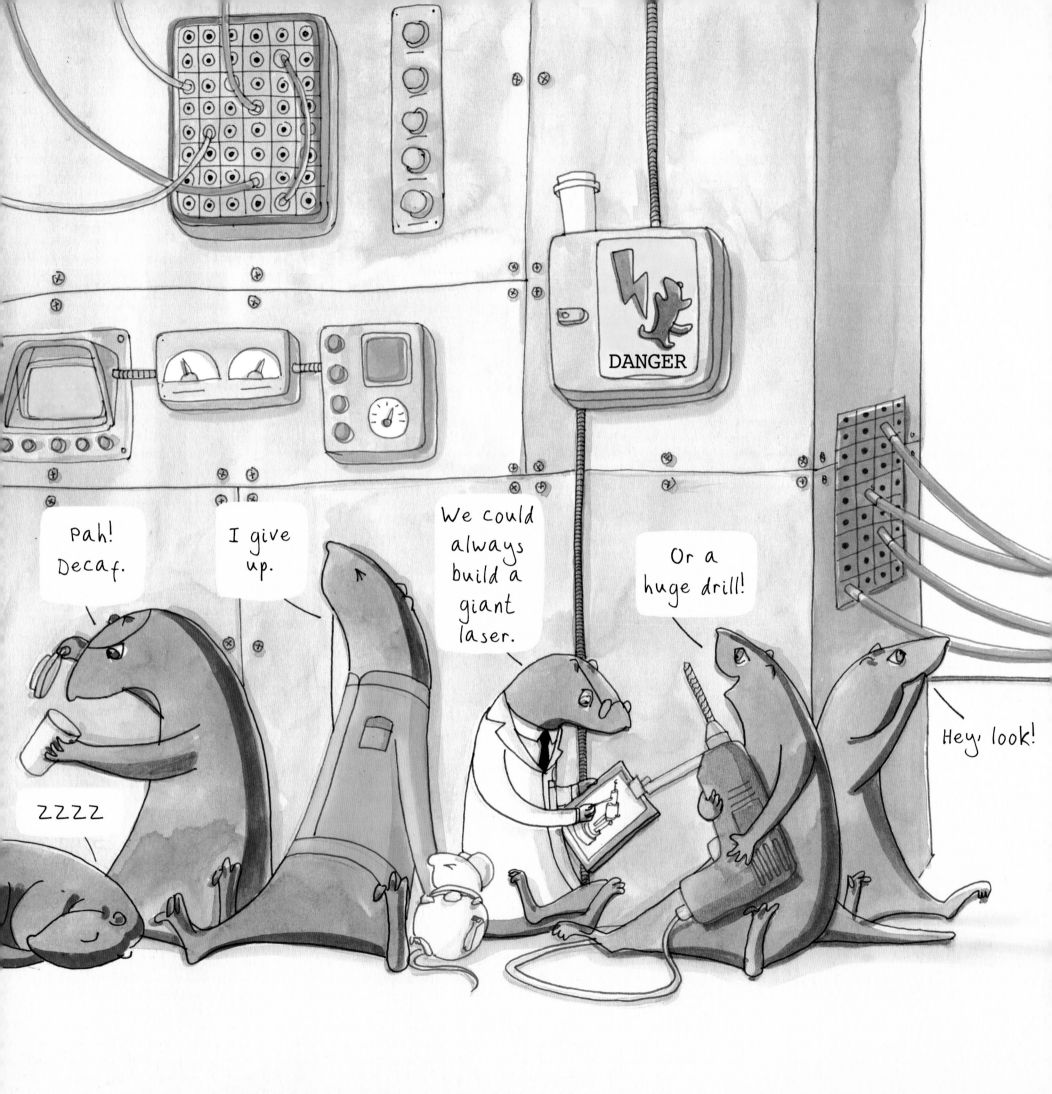

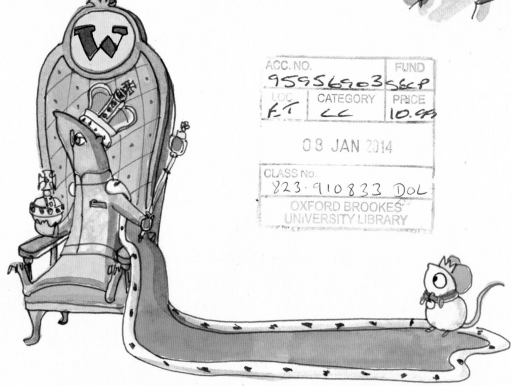